bindi
Wildlife Adventures

BOOK
3

BUSHFIRE!

BUSHFIRE!

Bindi Irwin

with Jess Black

sourcebooks
jabberwocky

Copyright © Australia Zoo 2010
Cover photograph © Australia Zoo
Cover and internal design by Christabella Designs
Cover and internal design © 2011 by Sourcebooks, Inc.

Published by Sourcebooks Jabberwocky, an imprint of Sourcebooks, Inc.
P.O. Box 4410, Naperville, Illinois 60567-4410
(630) 961-3900
Fax: (630) 961-2168
www.jabberwockykids.com

First published by Random House Australia in 2010.

Library of Congress Cataloging-in-Publication data is on file with the publisher.

Source of Production: Versa Press, East Peoria, IL, USA
Date of Production: April 2011
Run Number: 14964

Printed and bound in the United States of America.
VP 10 9 8 7 6 5 4 3 2 1

Dear Diary,

Things at home have been really hectic!

A bushfire in our local national park destroyed lots of animals' homes. Many animals were injured and needed our help. Everyone at the wildlife hospital worked around the clock.

There are so many stories to tell! Rosie and I went to help bring the injured animals back from the fire. Rosie cared for Spike the echidna, and I looked after the most beautiful koala called Smokey.

The day began normally, with a bushwalk up one of my favorite mountains...

Bindi

CHAPTER ONE

"I spy...a blue-tongue lizard!" cried Bindi, turning to her best friend, Rosie, and holding up her palm. "High-five, mate!"

The girls high-fived, giggling with excitement.

"That makes the score seven to us

and six to Richard. We are so going to win!" continued Bindi. The friends turned triumphantly to Rosie's dad, Richard, who was walking up the bush track behind them.

"There's an old saying, girls: don't count your chickens before they hatch," cautioned Richard. "In any case, unless you know the animal's scientific name, it doesn't count." He smiled, then strode past the girls, making his way farther up the mountain.

"That's not fair!" Bindi couldn't believe it. She had thought she and Rosie would finally beat Richard in a game of I Spy Wildlife.

"Dad, you're just trying to cheat because we're winning," said Rosie as she caught up to her father, with Bindi close behind.

"Two against one isn't fair either, but you don't see me accusing anyone of cheating." Richard looked at his daughter with a twinkle in his eye. "Nor do I think you *really* saw a rare spotted eagle about an hour ago. But as we have no video referee, I'll have to give you the benefit of the doubt."

Richard walked on, oblivious to the two friends exchanging glances and smiling. Was there anything Richard didn't know about animals? Some families played the regular game of I Spy but the Irwin and Bellamy families preferred their own animal-specific version. After all, they'd had lots of practice!

On this early morning, the three keen walkers were hiking up Mount Ngungun in the Glass House Mountains near Australia Zoo. It was one of Bindi's favorite things to do. She loved being outside and seeing animals in the wild. Bindi also loved hanging out with Rosie and Richard. Rosie's dad was strong and athletic and always up for anything. He especially liked to win at games and never lost on purpose to save hurt feelings. No, he was ruthless in his animal spotting and it made Bindi and Rosie all the more determined to beat him!

Bindi raced on and soon overtook Richard. She figured that if she and Rosie reached the lookout before him, they might have more chance of spotting animals. His height definitely put him at an advantage for seeing birds.

"Wait for me!" called Rosie as she caught up with Bindi. The two girls puffed as they scrambled toward the lookout. "Come on, Dad!"

"Good things come to those who wait!" said Richard as he continued on leisurely.

It was already a very hot day and the last steep push to the top was hard going. Bindi could feel the sweat trickling down her arms, her legs, and the back of her neck. They couldn't have done the hike any later on a day like this. They would risk heat exhaustion and dehydration, not to mention having zero chance of seeing any animals—they'd all have sensibly found refuge in the shade.

The girls were out of breath and red-faced by the time they reached the lookout. They both took big swigs from their water bottles.

"Look!" Bindi pointed to the other peak in the distance. "Mount

Tibrogargan looks just like King Kong!" The two friends marveled at the view of the majestic mountain peak to the east. They could see the sun coming up behind it, over the Pacific Ocean.

"Wow, it's really windy up here!" said Rosie, looking at the trees bending in the wind. It wasn't a refreshing breeze either, but a warm, blustery one.

Bindi spun around, taking in the view of the surrounding bush and mountain peaks. Something to the west caught her eye. "Oh no!"

"What is it?" asked Rosie and turned to see where Bindi was looking.

Bindi silently pointed into the distance.

The stunning view was obscured by a thick haze of smoke. The friends stared at each other in dismay.

Richard finally approached the top. His face and neck were wet with sweat. "What a day! It's got to be over 80 degrees already and it's only 8 a.m." He mopped his face.

"Dad, we've got some bad news," said Rosie.

Richard laughed. "Don't tell me, you've just seen three more animals and won the game?" He chuckled. "I can take defeat gracefully."

Rosie pointed, and Richard turned

to stare at the thick mass of smoke. Even as they watched, it grew darker and spread farther across the national park. The high temperatures and strong westerly winds were fanning the flames of a fire.

"Oh dear." Richard's expression was serious.

As head vet at the Australian Wildlife Hospital, Richard was well aware that a fire in this kind of bush could mean hundreds of displaced and injured animals, to say nothing of threatening the homes and property of people who lived in the area.

He turned to the friends with a grim expression on his face. "We'd better hurry back, girls. It'll be all hands on deck at the wildlife hospital." Richard took one last look at the fire and turned to make his way down the path at a brisk pace.

Bindi and Rosie hurried after the vet. All thoughts of their earlier game had vanished. The sooner they got to the hospital the better!

CHAPTER TWO

The Australian Wildlife Hospital was already humming with activity when the Bellamys and Bindi arrived. The staff was busy on the phones, and nurses moved rapidly down corridors. Richard disappeared almost immediately. He had plenty to do.

Rosie and Bindi had spent hours helping out at the hospital and knew what needed to be done in an emergency like this. The friends made their way toward the laundry. The staff would need plenty of extra bandages and clean towels folded and stacked at the ready. The girls worked quickly. After they had created a good stockpile of materials, they were eager to find more ways to help out.

Bindi was always amazed by the size of the hospital. There was a nursery for the baby animals, con- sultation rooms, treatment rooms, operating rooms, an intensive care unit, a pathology department, a pharmacy where all the medication was held, a staff room, and a kitchen. Richard was the main vet but there were six others who worked full-time in the hospital, loads of nurses, administration staff, and a huge number of volunteers, which the hospital depended on in order to survive. The hospital was open 24 hours a day and its policy was to never turn away an animal in need. It was a massive operation!

The girls found Richard and a couple of other staff members busily creating extra space in the conference room for animal patients.

Bindi shook her head in disbelief. "Do you really think we'll get this many injured animals?"

Richard shrugged. "Hopefully not, but it's better to be prepared. We won't have time to do this later on."

Richard's mobile rang. "Dr. Bellamy speaking." As Richard listened to the caller, he pulled out two bottles of water from a fridge and passed one to each of the girls.

"Got that. We've been waiting for your call. Thanks." Richard ended the phone call and slipped his mobile into his back pocket. Grabbing a few more bottles of water, he said, "Drink up, girls. You'll need to keep your fluids up. That was our official call to action."

The hospital was sending rescue teams to treat the animals that had been pulled from the fire. The animals would be given on-the-spot treatment before being brought back to the hospital. Bindi couldn't believe it! She would be going out on site to help animals right at the time they needed it most.

Richard rushed down the hospital corridor, heading for the rescue vehicle. Bindi and Rosie didn't need any more encouragement. "Animal rescue, here we come!"

With Richard at the wheel, Rosie and Bindi joined Tracy, a vet nurse, and Tanya and Joe, two volunteer carers, in the back of the van. Pretty soon they were out on the open road. The trees flashed past as they drove deeper into the national park.

As the van approached the fire, the smell of smoke grew stronger. Bindi coughed and her eyes started to sting. She squinted out the window at the charred bush to the side of the road. "It looks so awful," she whispered. The others nodded their agreement.

When they finally pulled up in a clearing, it felt as if they were very close to the fire; it was incredibly hot and ash swirled in the fierce wind. Bindi was glad they had brought so much extra drinking water. She already felt thirsty again.

A few tents had been hastily erected as a rest area for firefighters. People were shouting orders, massive pieces of fire-fighting equipment were being dragged this way and that, and there was so much smoke in the air that it was difficult to see.

Their small group gathered around Richard. "We can't go any closer to the fire; we leave that job to the professionals. This is an area where the firefighters can bring out any injured animals. Once we've looked them over and made them as comfortable as possible, we'll shuttle the animals back to the hospital."

Richard pointed to a small tent to the side. "We can set up our kit over here. The tent gives the animals some shade, which is vital. One of our first jobs will be to lower their body temperatures."

It didn't take long to unpack their emergency kit and get set up. Almost immediately, two animals were brought over for treatment. One was a little blue-tongue lizard with minor skin burns. Tracy took care of him by bathing him in cool water.

The other injured animal was a koala. He had large fluffy ears and a cute oversized nose. Even though he was hurt and distressed, Bindi thought he was the cutest, fattest koala she had ever seen. She was going to pay special attention to this little guy!

The firefighter who brought over the koala looked exhausted, and his face was smeared with black soot. Bindi quickly grabbed one of their water bottles and passed it to him. He nodded his thanks.

"Got our work cut out for us with this one, that's for sure," he grunted. "Terrible winds."

Bindi asked, "What's it like out there?"

The large man sighed. "It's not good. Hot and dangerous. But you know," he added, almost as an afterthought, "sometimes you can hold back the flames and then you really feel like you've made a difference." With that comment he was off again, running back toward the fire.

Bindi thought about his words.

She understood what he was talking about. Making a difference was what her family was all about.

Bindi and Rosie helped Richard hold the koala on the table while Richard injected him with some medicine to calm him down. He then put Bindi in charge of applying cooling pads to the koala's wounds. He explained that the koala had second-degree burns, which meant there was blistering on the skin. It was a serious injury. Richard looked worried.

As the poor creature became more sedated, Bindi was able to stroke his fur and talk gently to him.

"Don't worry, little fella. We'll take good care of you. Everything will be okay."

CHAPTER THREE

Terri and Robert were busy with worries of their own. Even though the fire was still some distance away, if it got out of control it could threaten the zoo. They had spent the morning going over the zoo's fire prevention procedures with Rosie's mum, Katie, who was one of the animal keepers. They had walked around the entire zoo looking over each enclosure.

Katie was reading through their evacuation plan one more time.

Robert turned to his mum. "What if the fire does come closer? What will we do?"

Terri smiled at her son. "Good question. Have you noticed all the big water tanks we have around the zoo?"

Robert nodded. "They're for our sprinkler system."

"That's right. We also have fire

hydrants we could use to help fight the fire."

Robert thought about this. "But what about the buildings? Could they burn down?"

"The buildings are all made from nonflammable materials, which means they don't catch fire easily."

Katie ticked off a few items from her list. "Don't forget we have the water trucks. And the zoo is also surrounded by firebreaks."

Terri nodded, satisfied. "It looks like we've done all we can. Of course, we can move the smaller animals if we have enough warning."

They wandered back through

the wallaby enclosure. Several rock wallabies were grazing lazily in the sun. They looked very content in their grassy home.

Suddenly Robert stopped walking. Something was troubling him. "But fires move really fast sometimes, don't they? What if we don't have much time?"

Terri shrugged. She looked meaningfully at Katie.

"It would be a very difficult decision. We'd have to weigh up the risk of evacuating versus staying."

Robert looked alarmed.

Terri tried to reassure her son. "If we did decide to stay, we'd make sure the animals had as much protection as possible."

Robert nodded soberly. "I hope we don't have to do that."

Terri and Katie shared a glance. They hoped so too. The fate of the zoo depended on it.

Richard had his hands full. More and more animals were being brought over to the emergency tent for treatment. It was devastating to see so many innocent native creatures injured and in pain from burns and smoke inhalation.

Richard checked up on Bindi and the koala she was nursing.

"I'm trying to think of a name for him. Any ideas?" Bindi asked him.

"How about Carol?" Richard suggested. "*She* has a little joey in her pouch."

Bindi's eyes widened. "That's why he's, I mean, *she's* so fat!"

Richard felt around the koala's abdomen. "The joey is still very young; she's not ready to come out yet."

Bindi realized she now had two

koalas to care for! "Will the joey be okay?"

"I hope so. We'll give it a full examination back at the hospital. Would you like to go back with the joey and her mum?"

Bindi nodded. "Definitely." There was no way this koala was going anywhere without her.

Bindi looked over at Rosie, who was caring for an echidna. The poor critter had lost a few spines, which had melted in the intense heat of the flames. Without them, he would be defenseless in the wild. He also had burns to the skin underneath his spines. Rosie was doing her best to make sure he was comfortable until they could get him back to the hospital.

"Have you thought of a name for the echidna yet?" Bindi asked her friend.

Rosie looked affectionately at the spiky creature. "I know it's not the most original name in the world but I'm calling him Spike. He's a tough little survivor, I just know it!" They chuckled quietly as they watched Spike's long tongue darting this way and that.

Bindi knew that Rosie felt as strongly about her patient as Bindi did about her koala. She looked down at the fluffy ears and the cuddly body of the koala mum fighting for her life. "I'm calling my koala Smokey. She's survived the fire and she's the color of smoke!"

The girls shared a smile. They were both a little scared by the bushfire but it felt good to be helping out.

"Come on, girls! Time to leave!" Richard's voice rang out over the noise. He was loading up the van with the most urgent cases.

"Come on, Smokey. Let's go back to the hospital and get you both well again. I promise to look after you." Bindi gave the sedated koala an affectionate pat.

Bindi and Rosie helped the others carry several animals over to the van. They were taking Smokey, Spike, an eastern gray kangaroo, a wallaby, four lizards, a brush-tailed possum, and a brown snake back to the hospital. It was a big responsibility to look after these animals but the girls were up to the task. Tracy, Tanya, and Joe were staying behind to care for the next load of incoming patients.

They were feeling that everything was under control when the rescue van turned a sharp corner and skidded to an abrupt halt.

Everyone was thrown sideways.

"Whoa!" Rosie called out. "What happened, Dad?"

Richard turned around to check on them. "Are you okay back there?"

"Yeah, we're fine. Just checking on the animals," said Rosie as she looked over the mini zoo in the back of the van.

Bindi nodded. "Yep, they're all fine."

Richard hopped out of the van, slamming the door in frustration. "I don't believe it!"

Bindi looked out of the windshield to see that an entire tree was lying across the road. The hot winds fanning the fire had blown over an old gum tree. It completely blocked their path.

This was really bad news!

Bindi called out to Richard. "Can we go a different way, Richard?"

Richard shook his head. "I'm afraid this is the only way out, Bindi."

Richard nudged the dead trunk with his foot. "We don't have time for this. These animals need help now."

Rosie and Bindi looked at each other, frightened. All around them was smoke and charred bush. They seemed too close to the fire here. The girls knew all of the animals in the back of the van were relying on them to stay alive. What could they do?

CHAPTER FOUR

Terri, Katie, and Robert were helping in the wildlife hospital when a voice came over the intercom.

"We've had a call from rescue van one. There's a tree down blocking their path and they need urgent assistance.

Critically injured animals need to get to the hospital as soon as possible."

Terri and Katie were already running to the reception area to get the details. Robert followed as fast as he could.

Terri called over her shoulder. "That'll be Richard, and he has the girls with him!"

They reached the reception. Terri called out to the staff member on the phone. "Tell him we're on our way. And we'll bring chain saws!"

Terri grabbed the keys for the second rescue van. She picked up the loudspeaker for the hospital intercom. "I need three volunteers who can use a chain saw to head out right now!"

In no time a small group was assembled and ready to go.

Robert tugged at Terri's sleeve. "Mum, Mum, I want to come too."

Terri smiled. "You're a brave kid, Robert Irwin. In you jump." She held the door open to the van as the volunteers and Robert jumped in the back.

"Let's go!" The van pulled out of the parking lot and they were away.

It was a tense wait for Richard, Bindi, and Rosie back near the fallen tree. The smoke was thick and the outside air temperature was super hot. It was uncomfortable just waiting in the van even with the air conditioning running. The animals really had to be kept cool.

Richard crouched in the back and moved from one animal to the next. He noticed that Bindi kept glancing out the front windshield to see if help had arrived yet.

"There's an old saying: a watched pot never boils. Let's keep busy. I need you both to help me while I tend to this roo. His injuries are serious, he's gone into shock, and his vital signs are dropping fast. I wanted to wait until we got back to the hospital but he needs help now."

Bindi was on the job. "What do you need us to do?"

Richard was busily sterilizing his hands as best he could. "Well, he's going to need some IV fluid."

Rosie and Bindi looked at him, wide-eyed.

"The surgery would have been better, but beggars can't be choosers. Come on, girls. Hop to it."

They sprang into action. Richard prepared a sterile area while giving orders to the girls to hand him instruments and help as much as possible while he attached the IV drip to the kangaroo. They watched anxiously.

Richard finished the operation and settled the kangaroo back into his crib. "We've helped this fellow out as much as we can for now, but he really needs to get to the hospital."

Rosie turned to her dad. "Do you know how the fire was started?"

He shook his head. "Well, nine times out of ten it's human carelessness. The firefighters suspect it was a campfire in a no-camping zone that got out of control."

"That's terrible. Why would anyone do that?" Rosie asked.

Richard shook his head. "I don't know. People need to stick to areas that have been set aside for camping. And on a total fire ban day, there is no way they should have been lighting fires." He turned his attention to a wallaby. "It's an even harder lesson for the animals. They have lost a home as well as a food supply. It will take months and months for the bush to grow back."

The loud toot of a horn got their attention. Bindi looked out the window to see the other rescue van pull up. Terri and Katie hopped out. Richard waved in relief.

"I don't think I've ever been so happy to see you both!" he called out.

Katie yelled back, "We're happy to be here."

"Are you girls okay?" Terri asked.

"We're fine, Mum," Bindi replied. "But we want to get these animals back to the hospital right away!"

Bindi and Rosie stayed in the van with the animals, watching the action through the front windshield. Terri, Katie, and the volunteers began their attack on the tree. Terri was giving instructions over the roar of the chain saws. They used chains attached to the four-wheel drive to begin hauling the large gum tree branches off the road.

It was then that Bindi noticed Robert looking around anxiously from the other van. She opened a window and called out to him. "G'day, Robert!"

Robert's face lit up. He waved furiously. Bindi waved back. Suddenly she felt a bit teary. It had already been a long, hard day and it was far from over.

Rosie knew exactly how Bindi was feeling. She leaned over and gave her best friend a big hug. "Don't worry, B. Our mums will have the tree cleared in no time and we'll make sure the animals get the help they need."

Bindi hugged her friend back. This was exactly what best friends were for!

CHAPTER FIVE

It was all systems go as the rescue van pulled into the animal hospital. The staff appeared from every corner of the hospital to help unload the animals. The kangaroo was moved onto a stretcher and carried inside, while the others could be moved in their cages.

Rosie and Bindi helped their adopted animals into the main reception area of the hospital. The narrow hall behind was immediately filled with animals needing attention.

"What will happen now?" Bindi asked Richard.

"Our triage nurse will inspect each animal and decide who needs to be seen right away and who can wait a little longer for more detailed treatment."

Richard pointed to the kangaroo. "Our courageous kangaroo will be the first cab off the rank."

Richard knew the girls were anxious about the animals they had adopted. "Try not to worry. Every animal will get the attention it needs. I'm not the only vet here. Your furry friends will be looked after."

Just then the front doors swung open, followed by a loud shout of "Incoming!"

A man covered in dirt and charcoal staggered up to the group. He held an injured possum in his arms. "This fellow needs help, doc."

"You both look as if you've been through the fire," said Richard, checking out man and possum.

"The fire came close to the back

of my land," the man explained. "I was hosing down my place when I caught a glimpse of this little bloke in the thick of it. He could hardly even move. It looks like he's burned his hands and feet."

Richard took a closer look at the wounds. "I can't believe he let you this close to him without anesthetic."

The man shook his head. He was just as surprised by the possum's actions. "I've never seen anything like it. He just seemed to know I'd do right by him."

Richard led the two of them to a consultation room. "Well, it sounds like you risked your life to save his.

I'm sure he's grateful. Let's take a look at him."

Bindi and Rosie hovered in the corridor, watching staff and volunteers whiz past. They weren't sure what to do next—everything had been such a whirlwind. Now here they were back at the hospital but all the staff had a fixed role and knew what job they were meant to be doing. All the girls wanted to do was help, but they didn't want to get in anyone's way.

Richard stuck his head back out into the corridor.

"Bindi! Rosie! I'll need your help, please! You know the old saying: many hands make light work!"

The girls couldn't help smiling at each other as they scuttled after Richard. He might like to overuse his old sayings, but he sure knew how to save lives.

Terri and Robert were helping out in the hospital kitchen preparing food and drinks for the staff and volunteers. They were making piles of sandwiches, a large pot of soup, a lasagne, and various salads. It was now midafternoon but many of the staff and volunteers would be working late into the night.

Bindi and Rosie wandered in, starving.

"You girls look like you need some food," said Terri as she dished out two plates of lasagne and salad and poured two glasses of lemonade.

"Thanks, Mum!"

"Thanks, Terri."

Bindi and Rosie plunked themselves down at the large table which dominated the room and wasted no time digging in.

Robert came over to the table, smiling. "I helped fry the meat."

53

Bindi smiled. "Mmmm, totally delicious, little buddy!" She was so grateful she didn't even mind when Robert stole a piece of cucumber from her plate.

He glanced out the window and frowned.

"What's up, Robert?" asked Rosie.

He was looking at the colorful wind socks that were flapping furiously outside the window. "D'you think the zoo's going to be okay with the fire and everything?"

Bindi and Rosie looked at the wind socks. "I think so. As long as the wind doesn't change direction," said Bindi.

The girls returned the plates to the kitchen and hurried back to surgery.

Terri came over and sat with Robert. "Thanks for your cooking expertise, Mr. Irwin," she said, ruffling his hair.

Robert was concentrating hard. He pointed to the fish-shaped wind sock. "Look at the wind sock, Mum. I don't think it was blowing in that direction before."

Terri froze as she watched it dancing like crazy in the wind.

Robert was right. The wind had changed direction. It would be bringing the fire directly in line with the zoo and the wildlife hospital.

CHAPTER SIX

Richard peered at Smokey's burns as she lay on the operating table under anesthetic. Bindi adjusted the surgical mask covering her nose and mouth and watched with interest as Richard talked her through the koala's treatment.

"Her burns are second degree, which means they are moderate but not beyond repair. We'll treat the burns, then pad and bandage her. We'll have to change the dressing daily."

He carefully reached inside Smokey's pouch and pulled out a tiny joey.

"Because the joey is only about four months old, she's what we call pre-pouch emergence. She's not ready to come out yet. We don't want to disturb her but we will need to check her and weigh her regularly to see if she's doing okay."

He took the tiny little koala and set her down on a set of scales. The vet nurse noted her weight.

"We'll also keep an eye on Smokey's milk supply. If her body shuts down due to her injuries then the joey will need a hand from us with a special koala formula we can make up."

He placed the tiny joey back into Smokey's pouch.

"It looks so snug in there," Bindi observed.

Richard finished cleaning up Smokey's burns and applied a dressing to the affected areas. "Now we need to X-ray Smokey to see if her lungs are clear."

The nurse took Smokey over to the X-ray room. As they waited for the results, Richard washed his hands. Bindi set about clearing the table.

Richard turned to her, his hands still dripping. "There's an old saying: all experience is education for the soul. Try to remember that, will you, in case things don't go the way you hope?"

Bindi nodded, a lump in her throat.

The nurse returned with the X-ray, which Richard held up to the light. After a long look he turned to Bindi. He pointed to Smokey's lungs on the X-ray. "See how the area is white? A clear lung would come up black on the X-ray."

Bindi looked at the picture. "That's not good, is it?"

Richard shook his head. "It's not great but it could still clear up before too much damage is done." Richard handed the X-ray back to the nurse.

Bindi felt tears prick at her eyes. All she wanted to do was help Smokey but she didn't know how.

Richard said gently, "I've got another operation to do now. I'll let you know about Smokey as soon as we know anything more. In the meantime, Tracy is going to show you how to tend to Smokey so she's as comfortable as possible. Could you do that for me, Bindi?"

Bindi cleared her throat. "Of course."

Bindi listened as Tracy gave her instructions for the koala's care. She would do everything she could for this beautiful little animal!

CHAPTER SEVEN

Richard re-sterilized and entered another operating room. The team was waiting for him. They were preparing to operate on Spike, the little echidna. Some of his spikes needed to be removed.

Rosie was helping her dad by holding the anesthetic mask over the echidna's face.

"The echidna's spines provide such good protection. In this case too much protection. We need to get to the burns on his skin underneath."

Rosie leaned in closer to watch her dad. "How will Spike manage without his spines?"

"Don't worry, Rosie, there's an old saying: beauty is only skin deep. We'll have this little fellow back up and running around in no time. His spines will grow back in about a year."

Richard peered down at the

tangle of spines. "Now, here comes the tricky part."

Richard was poised to begin the extraction. Everyone leaned forward to watch just as the room was plunged into darkness. There was a collective groan from everyone in the room.

"Uh oh! Power out! In this kind of heat the grid gets overloaded." Richard paused. "The generator should have cut in by now. Julie, can you please go see what's going on?"

Nurse Julie felt her way toward the drawer where the flashlights were kept. She turned one on and handed it to Rosie and took another one with her. "I'll be back as soon as I can."

Richard became aware of the shuffling of feet. "Everyone else stay as still as possible and don't touch anything. We want the area to remain sterile."

There was an uncomfortable silence as everyone tried not to move in the pitch black. Richard's voice cut through the tension. "Anyone know any good ghost stories?"

Rosie couldn't believe her father. "Dad! You're in the middle of an operation!" But then she remembered a funny joke she had heard at school. "Okay, I know a ghost joke. Why are ghosts so bad at telling jokes?" She shone her flashlight into the others' faces. Everyone shook their heads. "Because you can see right through them!"

They all chuckled.

Clare, the other nurse, piped up. "Oh, I've got one. What's a ghost's favorite dessert? Boo-berry pie and I scream!"

More chuckles before a flashlight flickered in the doorway and Julie came back into the room.

"The generator hasn't kicked in due to the heat, so they're trying to manually restart it. We might not get the power back for some time."

"Okay then. We'll have to keep going by flashlight." Richard turned to his daughter. "Rosie, I'll need you to hold your flashlight for me over Spike. They're not sterile so you won't be able to touch anything else. Julie, please shine yours here too."

Richard leaned forward toward the little echidna and began extracting his spines…by flashlight.

CHAPTER EIGHT

Hours later, Richard found Bindi and Rosie curled up fast asleep on the couch in the staff room.

He turned on a light and gently shook them both awake.

"Sorry to wake you, girls." He

gave them a moment to take in their surroundings.

"What time is it?" asked Rosie groggily.

Richard checked his watch. "It's after 10 p.m."

"The power's back on," Rosie noted.

Richard nodded. "They managed to fix the generator about an hour ago."

Bindi's first thought was the koala and her joey. "How's Smokey?"

Richard sat down on the couch between Rosie and Bindi. "That's what I wanted to talk to you about. We performed another X-ray on Smokey's lungs and they're not improving. She's developed an infection."

He paused before he continued. "She has pneumonia, Bindi. I'm afraid it means she won't get better."

Bindi tried to take in the news. She felt numb. Rosie squeezed her friend's hand in sympathy.

"Would you like to say good-bye to her?" asked Richard softly.

Bindi nodded furiously. Richard led the way into one of the operating rooms.

Smokey was lying on the table, her eyes half open. Bindi could feel tears start to fall down her cheeks. "She looks so peaceful."

"She's been sedated. The good news is we're going to be able to save the joey. She's very young but we can raise her in the nursery. She's going to need lots of care, Bindi. Do you think you could take her on as a special patient?"

Bindi approached the table and looked at Smokey. Bindi gently stroked her fur. "I promise I'll take good care of your baby, Smokey."

It was as if the koala mother knew that Bindi would look after her joey. She opened her big brown eyes and blinked. She trusted Bindi. Bindi had helped her when she had been scared and in pain. She couldn't feel the pain anymore.

Richard carefully removed the joey from Smokey's pouch.

"We need to get the little one settled in the nursery. She'll need a heat lamp and an incubator. Now's the time to say good-bye to Smokey."

Richard left the room with the joey.

Smokey had Bindi's finger grasped in her paw. "Sleep tight, Smokey."

Bindi gave Smokey one last look, gently pulled her finger away, and left the room. Despite her tears, Bindi knew she would need to be strong to look after Smokey's joey.

And Bindi was a friend who always kept her promises.

CHAPTER NINE

Half an hour later, the intercom crackled to life around the hospital. A voice called out in a state of high excitement. "We have just received news that it is raining in the area surrounding the fire. I repeat, IT IS

RAINING HARD, and authorities believe the fire will shortly be under control. Congratulations, guys, the worst is over!"

There were cheers throughout the hospital. The staff celebrated with a small party in the kitchen, drinking leftover lemonade and eating cookies.

Everyone was exhausted. Bindi and Rosie munched away while Richard held up a cup of lemonade and called for silence.

"Thanks to everyone for their hard work. It's been a tough day, and animal lives have been lost," said Richard as he glanced over at

Bindi. "But we've also *saved* a lot of lives today too. I'd especially like to thank our volunteers." He looked out at the sea of tired faces. "We'd be lost without your help."

Everyone held up their glasses.

"Cheers!"

CHAPTER TEN

Bindi had been to the hospital twice a day, every day, for the past week to visit the koala joey in the nursery.

The little koala had taken to the special formula and was fast asleep in her incubator. Bindi watched her as she slept. She looked just like any baby, apart from the exceptionally cute furry ears—just like her mum's, thought Bindi.

Bindi was about to head out when Richard walked in. He smiled when he saw the little joey curled into a ball. "We're very pleased with the joey's progress."

"She's looking great," said Bindi as she unzipped her bag and pulled out a rolled-up poster. "I made something for you, Dr. Richard." She handed it to him.

Richard slowly unrolled the cardboard to reveal a colorful hand-drawn poster. He read out:

To Dr. Richard. There's an old saying: be the change you want to see in the world. It reminds us of you. Thank you. Love from all the staff and animal patients at the Australian Wildlife Hospital.

The poster was covered in signatures and paw prints.

Richard was touched. "Thanks, Bindi. That's going straight onto my wall in my office so I can look at it every day." He nodded thoughtfully. "Great saying. I'll be sure to use that one at the first opportunity!"

Bindi giggled. "I know you will!"

Dr. Richard chuckled as the two

wandered back down the corridors of the wildlife hospital and out into the sunshine.

THE KOALA

- Koalas are not bears! They are actually marsupials that carry their young in a pouch.

- Koalas are found in eucalyptus forests around the eastern and southeastern coast of Australia.

- The koala's main food source, eucalyptus, does not provide a lot of energy, and for this reason koalas sleep up to 20 hours a day.

🐾 "Koala" is commonly thought to have come from an Australian Aboriginal word meaning "no drink," referring to koalas only occasionally having to drink water.

🐾 Koalas have a great sense of hearing and an even better sense of smell. This is how they select which leaves are the best to eat.

🐾 When a female koala is ready to breed she will call out to a male by letting out a loud snorting bellow. The female gives birth 35 days after mating.

🐾 When born, the baby koala weighs only half a gram and is the size of a kidney bean and less than an inch long. Its eyes open at 22 weeks and it grows teeth at 24 weeks.

ANIMAL FACT FILE

THE ECHIDNA

- The echidna is part of the monotreme family, and they are egg-laying mammals. The only other monotreme in the world is the platypus.

- Found throughout Australia, the echidna is a highly adaptable creature and can be found in coastal forests, alpine meadows, and interior deserts.

- The echidna has distinctive sharp spines (quills) along its back and sides for protection against predators.

- The echidna's tongue is approximately 7 inches long.

- Echidnas have no teeth! They live on a very specific diet of termites, ants, and other soil invertebrates, especially beetle larvae.

- The echidna's breeding season occurs during July and August. After mating, the male and female go their separate ways. Four weeks later, the female lays a single egg into a pouch on her abdomen. Ten days later the baby echidna hatches and starts to lap up milk from its mother.

Become a
Wildlife Warrior!

Find out how at
www.wildlifewarriors.org.au

Become a friend of wildlife.
Make sure you report any
person you see mistreating
animals, especially our native
wildlife, to the police.

COMING NOVEMBER 2011

bindi Wildlife Adventures
An EXCITING adventure story!
BOOK 4
CAMOUFLAGE

bindi Wildlife Adventures
An EXCITING adventure story!
BOOK 5
A WHALE OF A TIME

bindi Wildlife Adventures
An EXCITING adventure story!
BOOK 6
ROAR!

The adventures continue in

BOOK
4

CAMOUFLAGE

CHAPTER ONE

Bindi stared into the shop window, paying close attention to a gorgeous multicolored shoulder bag. "Check out that bag, Mum," she said enthusiastically. "It's so pretty!"

Robert wasn't too far away,

staring with undisguised admiration at a toy shop, which had boxes and boxes of remote-controlled dinosaurs just waiting to be bought.

"Mum, look at the velociraptor!" he said, awestruck. "It looks so real."

Bindi was now peering closely at the price tag on the bag, looking worried. "Um, are Singapore dollars more or less than Australian dollars?"

Terri laughed. "Less." She glanced at the price tag. "But not that much less!" She dragged her kids away from the enormous shopping area that was a part of Singapore's Changi Airport. "C'mon you two, ignore the shopping and let's head toward the baggage claim. Dr. Timothy will be waiting for us."

Dr. Timothy Chan was an old friend of the Irwins'. He had worked as a reptile keeper at Australia Zoo for three years, and was now based back in his home country. In two days' time he'd be opening a brand new reptile park on the beautiful island of Pulau Ubin.

The Irwins had been invited by Dr. Timothy to attend the official opening of the park. So not only were they excited about seeing Dr. Timothy again, they were going to see a whole lot of reptiles, which was doubly exciting.

After grabbing their luggage, the Irwins went through to the arrivals hall and, as promised, Dr. Timothy was there, a big smile on his face.

"Terri, Bindi, Robert! Welcome to Singapore!" He gave them all a hug. "You kids are getting bigger and stronger every time I see you. You'll be helping your mum catch crocodiles in no time."

Bindi was keen to set her friend straight. "We already do, Dr. Timothy."

Robert was not going to be left out. "Me too. Last time we went on a croc research trip, I helped too."

Dr. Timothy smiled. "Now why

doesn't that surprise me? Well, you kids will come in very handy at the Pulau Ubin Reptile Park," he said. "We've got a few crocs, a few goannas, three sailfin lizards, four different species of frogs, salamanders, rainforest dragons, and of course, we have—"

"Komodo dragons!" Bindi and Robert finished his sentence for him.

The Komodo dragon was Dr. Timothy's favorite reptile. The largest lizard in the world had been an obsession of his since he was a young boy. He had learnt everything he could about the lizards, and was now one of the world's foremost authorities on the creature. No one knew more about Komodo dragons than Dr. Timothy!

"Well, let's get out of the airport. I thought I'd take you straight to the island so you can have a look around." Timothy looked at the Irwins, who were nodding enthusiastically. "Unless you're feeling tired, and I should take you to your hotel first?"

"No way! We want to see your reptiles!"

"I thought you might say that." He grinned. "Well, it's an interesting ride. I'll drive us to the ferry terminal and from there we can take a bumboat over to the island."

Robert grinned from ear to ear. "Did you say bumboat?"

Timothy directed his guests out of the terminal and into the humid Singapore air of the car park. "Yes, a bumboat. They're traditional barges that have been used around the islands and on the Singapore River for hundreds of years. They're also called *tongkangs* or *twakows*."

Bindi couldn't let the joke end there. "Will we be traveling by bumcar, Dr. Timothy? Or bumcycle?"

Robert snorted with laughter, and Bindi dissolved into giggles.

Terri just looked at her kids. "Sorry, Timothy. My children are...

well, children, and any word with bum in it seems to be too darn funny for words."

He smiled at the kids, who were still doubled up with laughter. "Ah, I'm afraid this word is so familiar to me, I didn't realize it could also be funny." He considered it for a moment. "Yes, I guess it is sort of humorous."

He pointed in the direction of his car, and the four walked toward it.

"Here we are." Dr. Timothy grabbed their luggage and piled it into the boot. Unlocking the doors, he gestured to the Irwins. "Your *bum*station-wagon awaits."

CHAPTER TWO

The ferry ride out to Pulau Ubin was short, but it was a refreshing journey after being cooped up in an airplane for so long. The scenery was beautiful. Dr. Timothy pointed out the pretty Changi coastal areas, and the coastline and mountainous regions of nearby Malaysia. The tranquillity was often interrupted by enormous jets flying overhead, but it all added to the excitement of the place. They were a world away from Australia Zoo, and it felt like an adventure was about to begin!

The ferry terminal was a hive of activity. There was another bumboat already docked, and couriers leaped on and off three smaller boats, unloading boxes and various equipment onto the wharf.

Dr. Timothy looked on, scratching his head in amazement. "I can't believe we're so close to opening.

I've been working toward this for so many years."

Terri smiled at her old friend. "And we're thrilled to be here to watch it happen, Timothy."

Timothy turned to the kids. "Are you ready for the tour?"

"You bet!" they chorused.

Timothy began to guide them toward the entrance gate, where workmen were putting the finishing touches to the admissions desk. "Okay then, I think we should start with the amphibian exhibit over—"

"Timmy, Timmy, come over here, darling," interrupted a woman's shrill voice.

Dr. Timothy visibly sagged at the sound. He pasted a smile on his face and turned to his guests. "Ah, I must introduce you to our esteemed patron."

"Well, well, this must be the famous Irwin family. How nice of you to visit our little island," said the small woman with the extremely large voice. She tottered over to them on her high heels. She wore an expensive-looking leather jacket and skirt, and her sleek black hair was scraped back in a tight bun.

"Terri, Bindi, Robert. May I introduce you to Mrs. Cynthia Yeoh."

The Irwins subconsciously moved away from Cynthia Yeoh rather than toward her. "G'day, Mrs. Yeoh." Bindi tried to be polite, but there was just something a little "ick" about the woman.

Terri put out her hand to shake Cynthia's, but Cynthia moved in and gave all three of them a hug. It was the most unwelcoming limp hug any of them had ever experienced. Her clothes were cold to the touch. It was almost like she was wearing…

"Ewww, are you wearing snakeskin?" Robert screwed up his face at the thought.

Cynthia let out a high-pitched

laugh. "Of course I am, darling boy. If I can't wear snakeskin at a reptile park, where can I wear it?" She laughed again.

The Irwins didn't share her sense of humor, and looked at Dr. Timothy, speechless.

He tried to smooth things over. "Cynthia has helped us raise funds and awareness for the reptile park," he explained. "Her husband, Mr. Jack Yeoh, is Minister of Planning and the Environment—"

"It's true, but everyone knows I do all the work around here!" Her shrill laugh filled the air again.

Robert couldn't help himself. He

put his hands over his ears. She would give a flock of galahs a headache!

Dr. Timothy continued. "Yes, she has been extremely helpful. And—"

"And tomorrow night I'm hosting *the* social highlight of the Singaporean calendar!" She gave a grand sweeping gesture, as if she was addressing a theatre full of people.

"Oh, that's nice," Terri said. She turned to Dr. Timothy to ask him to begin the tour of the grounds, but Cynthia interrupted once more.

"It's for the opening of the park, of course, and there will be a traditional Chinese banquet at my home. A who's who of the Singaporean social scene will be there. My husband is away on business, but everyone else will be there. And media—there will be *tons* of media! You will be my guests of honor. I won't take no for an answer." Her head swiveled round as she caught sight of a passing employee. "Rupert," she screeched to him. "Get one of the boys to empty his boat. I need to get back to the mainland pronto!"

She tottered off toward the ferry with a dismissive wave to Timothy and the Irwins, who felt like they'd just been hit by a mini tornado.